IN THE FOOTSTEP

THE CASE OF THE
BUCHANAN CURSE

A new Sherlock Holmes story based on the
notebooks and papers of John H. Watson MD

Written and Researched by
ALLEN SHARP

Cambridge University Press
Cambridge
New York   Port Chester   Melbourne   Sydney

In the footsteps of Sherlock Holmes
The Case of the Baffled Policeman
The Case of the Buchanan Curse
The Case of the Devil's Hoofmarks
The Case of the Frightened Heiress
The Case of the Gentle Conspirators
The Case of the Howling Dog
The Case of the Man who Followed Himself
The Case of the Silent Canary

Published by the Press Syndicate of the University of Cambridge
The Pitt Building, Trumpington Street, Cambridge CB2 1RP
40 West 20th Street, New York, NY 10011, USA
10 Stamford Road, Oakleigh, Melbourne 3166, Australia

First published 1990

Printed in Great Britain by the Guernsey Press Co. Ltd, Guernsey

British Library cataloguing in publication data
Sharp, Allen
The case of the Buchanan Curse
I. Title   II. Series
823'.914[F]

ISBN 0 521 38955 0   DS

The cover photograph is reproduced with permission from
City of Westminster: Sherlock Holmes Collection, Marylebone Library
The picture frame was loaned by Tobiass.
pp.34–5 by Celia Hart
p.88 Royal Commission on Ancient Monuments, Scotland

The author wishes to acknowledge the indispensable
assistance which has been afforded by frequent reference
to the considerable earlier work of the late
Sir Arthur Conan Doyle.

About the Series

In 1881, Sherlock Holmes, while working in the chemical laboratory of St Bartholomew's hospital in London, met Dr John Watson, an army surgeon recently returned to England. Watson was looking for lodgings. Holmes had just found some which were too large for his needs, and wanted someone to share the rent. So it was that Holmes and Watson moved into 221B Baker Street. It was the beginning of a partnership which was to last more than twenty years and one which would make 221B Baker Street one of the most famous addresses in all of England.

Some credit for that partnership must also go to Mrs Hudson, Sherlock Holmes' landlady and housekeeper. It was she who put up with a lodger who made awful smells with his chemical experiments, who played the violin at any time of the day or night, who kept cigars in the coal scuttle, and who pinned his letters to the wooden mantlepiece with the blade of a knife!

So it is perhaps not unfitting that the only original documents which are known to have survived from those twenty years are now owned by Mrs Susan Stacey, a grandniece of that same Mrs Hudson. They include three of Dr Watson's notebooks or, more accurately, two notebooks and a diary which has been used as a notebook. The rest is an odd assortment, from letters and newspaper clippings to photographs and picture postcards. The whole collection has never been seen as anything more than a curiosity. The notebooks do not contain any complete accounts of cases – only jottings – though some of these were very probably made on the spot in the course of actual investigations. Occasionally, something has been pinned or pasted to a page of a notebook. There are some rough sketches and, perhaps the most interesting, there are many ideas and questions which Watson must have noted down so that he could discuss them with Holmes at some later time.

But now, by using Watson's notebooks, old newspaper reports, police files, and other scraps of information which the documents provide, it has been possible to piece together some of Holmes' cases which have never before been published. In each story, actual pages from the notebooks, or other original documents, have been included. They will be found in places where they add some information, provide some illustration, or pick out what may prove to be important clues.

But it is hoped that they also offer something more. By using your imagination, these pages can give **you** the opportunity to relive the challenge, the excitement and, occasionally, the danger which Watson, who tells the stories, must himself have experienced in working with Sherlock Holmes – the man so often described as "the world's greatest detective".

Chapter One

Four Centuries of Murder

Among the many strange episodes that I encountered in my long association with Sherlock Holmes, I would consider the story I am about to relate as among the most bizarre and frightening. Yet upon rereading my notes, written many years ago, I am struck by one curious fact. If I were now asked what aspect of the case I considered to be the most remarkable, then I'd have to answer, "That I allowed myself to become involved in it in the first place!"

It was not a time at which Holmes and I were still sharing the lodgings in Baker Street. In the previous year, I had married Mary Morstan and bought a small medical practice in the Paddington area. I felt that the world could offer me nothing more than I already had – the devotion of a dear wife and the satisfaction of pursuing the profession which I most loved.

Had anyone then suggested that I could be lifted out of that ideal world for the purpose of embarking upon some outlandish expedition, unsure even of the reasons for it, I would have thought them insane. Yet it did happen and, since even now I find it difficult to account logically for my actions, I can do no more than relate the sequence of events which led to them.

....

As I began my Monday morning surgery at Praed Street on October 1st 1888, I had no reason to suppose that there would be anything unusual about it. There were a dozen patients in the waiting room. Most of them were regulars, some of them sufficiently well acquainted with their ailments to feel confident enough to do their own diagnosis and prescription – "It's the stomach again, doctor. It'll be the brown bottle with the white sentiment that has to be shook. If I can have the big size, then it'll likely save me coming back."

It was only after I'd seen the first three that I began to suspect that perhaps all was not quite as usual. Each patient had shown rather less concern with whatever ailed them, than with what they obviously saw as a golden opportunity to obtain some knowledgeable answers upon the anatomy of the female abdomen. This sudden interest of my patients in such an unlikely subject wasn't so extraordinary as it may sound. It was, indeed, something which I should have foreseen.

The cause was a series of particularly horrific

murders, the first of which had taken place as far back as April of that year, though three more had occurred before they were to be connected. That was in early September, and it is no exaggeration to say that since that time London had been experiencing something of a sense of panic. All four murders had taken place in the East End of London, in the vicinity of Aldgate and the Whitechapel Road. All of the victims had been women, and all of them prostitutes. It might be supposed that such events would be of no great concern to the residents of, let us say, Westminster, or Paddington, and certainly not a matter likely to cause "panic". But September is the month in which the London fogs begin, nightly covering the capital in a frightening blanket of near impenetrable darkness. Even sounds become strangely muffled, their direction deceptive. But there was no mistaking the cries of the newspaper sellers on the night the evening edition of the *Star* carried the front page story, "Horrible Whitechapel Murders". And so, each night, it went on: "Whitechapel Murders – Latest. Police Baffled"; "Maniac Killer Still At Large". Somewhere a mad killer walked in the fog-bound darkness. The police were "baffled". The killer would surely strike again. No-one knew when. Nor could any Londoner feel certain where!

The killer *had* struck again, twice, in the early hours of yesterday morning, Sunday, September 30th. There were now six victims. Three had suffered savage mutilations to the abdomen.

Whilst therefore understanding the reason for my patients' morbid curiosity, I had no intention of satisfying it. That did not prevent my finishing surgery very late. It had been my intention to return home before setting out on my round of morning house calls. I could still have gone straight out on my calls, but the hour was so late, I decided to return home and begin my calls after an early lunch. I remember regarding it, at the time, as a fortunate choice, for I arrived home to discover that we had a visitor who, having already waited an hour, was about to leave. That visitor was Sherlock Holmes.

Holmes and I had seen little of each other since my marriage and I was naturally delighted to see him. Having exchanged the obvious if none the less sincere pleasantries, I explained the reason for my lateness. I remarked that I had been surprised not to see Holmes' name mentioned in the newspapers in connection with these terrible crimes, though I felt certain that he must have been receiving very frequent visits from his friends at Scotland Yard.

"I have seen Lestrade, quite recently," Holmes replied, "though not in connection with the Whitechapel Murders. That investigation is entirely in the hands of Chief Inspector Abbeline, working, I'm told, under the personal supervision of Commissioner Warren. As you know, Watson, Abbeline and I have little time for each other. As to Commissioner Warren, I do not see his approaching me for assistance. I've had no personal dealings with the man, but I'm sure he's aware of my differences with his predecessor, Henderson, and with Monro over my part in the investigation of the Fenian bombings (*The Case of the Silent Canary*). But I didn't come here to talk about myself. Tell me what you've been doing."

"Nothing," I said, "nothing that you could possibly see as other than dull. Treating my patients' aches and pains, and otherwise enjoying a quiet married life."

Mary interrupted, first to enquire whether Holmes would stay to lunch and, second, to tell me that she had already mentioned to Sherlock what she called, "the odd business in Edinburgh". Since Holmes *was* staying, Mary then excused herself to see to matters in the kitchen.

"I trust, Watson, that you are going to tell me all about the 'odd business in Edinburgh'."

It was not a matter that I would have thought to mention, but Mary had now left me little alternative. I asked Holmes what he already knew.

"Only that it is something you've heard from an old army friend – McIntyre. I do remember the name, and your receiving the occasional letter from him when we were together at Baker Street."

Holmes was correct in his recollection. James McIntyre was a friend from my time in the Afghan War. I, of course, was wounded and had been forced to return to England. McIntyre had resigned his commission two years later and returned to Scotland to take over his father's practice in Edinburgh. We had not actually met since our time together in the army, but we had continued to correspond regularly.

"It's really only a piece of foolishness," I said. "You might say that it has the makings of a good anecdote. I'm certain that McIntyre had no intention of its being taken seriously."

"Watson, I'll not pretend that I don't miss your company. Since you left Baker Street, life seems never to be anything other than serious. I think that I could enjoy a good anecdote, even a piece of 'foolishness'."

Since I appeared to have run out of excuses to avoid the issue, I set about trying to put McIntyre's long and somewhat rambling account into some sort of logical sequence, of which I hoped Holmes would not be too critical.

McIntyre, and his father before him, had attended over some sixty years to the medical needs of an Edinburgh family called Buchanan. There was now only one Buchanan, Athol, a man of forty-three, unmarried and without heirs, likely therefore to be the last of that particular branch of the Buchanan family. The name is not uncommon in Scotland.

Other than the usual childhood diseases, Athol Buchanan appeared never to have ailed anything and, in the years McIntyre had been in the practice, he'd had no occasion to visit the Buchanan

house, other than to tend to the needs of two age-
ing servants. It was for that purpose he'd paid a
recent visit, a visit on which he had been surprised and somewhat disturbed to find Athol
Buchanan in a state of alcoholic stupor, not, he
was told, the result of some temporary indiscre-
tion, but of a bout of heavy drinking that had
begun weeks before and was, if anything becoming more excessive.

McIntyre, concerned that the cause of this
hitherto unknown behaviour might be something
upon which he could offer help or advice, had
succeeded in sobering the man up at least to a
point where he could question him and obtain
understandable answers. Understandable, the
answers may have been, but rational, they most
certainly were not.

Buchanan had explained to McIntyre that the
reason for his unusual behaviour was really quite
simple. In a few weeks' time, he would be dead.
That, he saw as quite inevitable. "They say,
Doctor," Buchanan had said, "that when you
leave this world, you can't take anything with
you. I am endeavouring to prove 'them' wrong.
Over the years, I've sold everything of value in
this house. I've very little money. But what I do
have left in this world is the dwindling remains of
what was once a good wine cellar. It is that which I
intend to take with me!"

"Naturally," I told Holmes, "McIntyre had assumed that the man was still intoxicated and

couldn't be held accountable for such obvious fantasy. All that was certain was that if he could not stop him drinking to such excess, the fantasy might well become reality! He had told the servants to lock the wine cellar and 'lose' the key, promising to return the next day."

McIntyre's second visit had, if anything, proved more surprising than the first. He had expected one of two possible situations. If the man had somehow regained access to the contents of the cellar he would be in much the same state as McIntyre had found him on the previous day. If he had not, then he would be sober – but doubtless enraged by what he would see as McIntyre's inexcusable interference in matters which were arguably none of his concern.

In the event, neither proved to be the case. The man was sober, but not in ill temper. He confessed that, in truth, the bottle had done nothing to ease his torment of mind. Perhaps nothing would, yet McIntyre's visit had left him with a sense of sudden calm, maybe only of resignation, but of something which he had not experienced in many months.

"Yesterday," Buchanan said, "I told you something which I have told to no man. In doing it, it felt as if some burden had been lifted from my mind. You cannot prevent what is to happen, but if it is truly your wish to help me, then listen to my story."

McIntyre could hardly refuse.

In the sixteenth century, the Buchanans were a wealthy Scottish family, owning lands in Lothian, which at that time stretched south from the Forth to the Cheviot Hills of Northumberland. The Register of the Great Seal of Scotland shows that in 1507 the Buchanans acquired as landowning neighbours the brothers George and John *Faw* (or *Faa*), who variously described themselves as "Dukes" or "Earls" of Egypt. In later times, they would have been called "gypsies", a name which itself derives from the word Egyptian. Much is known about the Faws and their kin, not least from the Council Registers of the City of Aberdeen where such was the "annoyance" caused by petty thieving on the part of the "Egyptians" that an edict was passed banning them from the town.

It was an edict never to be enforced since, for reasons which remain uncertain, the then king of Scotland, James V, promptly agreed a treaty between himself and John Faw "Lord and Earl of Little Egypt". It was a treaty which, in effect, gave independence to the Egyptians living within the Scottish realm and the right to live by and enforce their own laws and customs. They were to be assisted in so doing by the representatives of the king's justice.

If uncertainty remains as to the reason for James' action, one man had no doubt of it – the then laird of the Buchanan lands, Donald Buchanan. The Egyptians were, he declared, "liars, thieves, and vagabonds all. Only by means of deceipt and falsehood, in which they were most clearly skilled, could they have fooled the king into this royal madness."

The growing frustration of Donald Buchanan can, at least, be understood when, despite frequent excursions onto the Buchanan lands by Egyptians apparently bent on theft, any action he might have taken against them was invariably thwarted by the king's protection. But of one thing, Donald Buchanan was to become increasingly aware. The hand of genius behind the activities of the Egyptians, at least in that region, was neither a Faw nor one of their acolytes. It was a woman, and one of a most striking appearance. Only in having black eyes did she resemble the others of her people, for she was fair skinned and with hair which was snow white and hung down her back in straight tresses of remarkable length. Her name was *Dya*, a word which means "mother". Dya had the "gift". She could read the Tarot and the stars. She could see a man's future in his hand and change those things which were not already ordained.

There is among the gypsies, even today, a thing which is called *mochardi*. It cannot be translated. Some will say it means "unclean" – but not in the sense of "dirty" or "infectious". It is a part of the gypsy religion which determines that at certain times, women are expelled from their community to live alone for whatever period the custom may require. Dya was not excluded from this practice.

It was for that reason that she was to wander alone onto Buchanan land and to be confronted by none other than Donald Buchanan. What took place at that meeting is recorded only in its final tragic outcome. Donald Buchanan strangled the woman Dya with her own hair.

Donald Buchanan and his family fled the country for France. His lands, he left to the charge of others of his kin, but they did not prosper.

"Always," Buchanan said, "they were in the wrong place at the wrong time, and on the wrong side. The last male of that Scottish family died at Culloden in the final Jacobite uprising. But there was still a penalty to pay – the loss of the last of the Buchanan lands."

"And these misfortunes," McIntyre suggested, "you associate with the killing of this gypsy woman – you might say, as if a curse had been placed upon the Buchanan family."

"You are both right and wrong, Doctor," was Buchanan's answer. "There was indeed a curse, but not one of which I have yet told you. I said that the woman Dya could foresee the future. She foresaw the exact time and the manner of her own death, and left behind her a paper to prove it. It was in that paper that she spelled out the curse. The paper itself no longer exists. I cannot therefore vouch for the exact words, but of the intention there is no doubt. It was that the man who took her life, and the first-born male of each succeeding generation would live no longer than she, her age being two full moons past two score years and three. And if any should reach that age, then the manner of their death would be as was her own. Doctor, I am the first-born of my father. I have just passed my forty-third birthday. Two full moons from now is the ninth day of November – the day that I shall die. The manner of my death will not be pleasant, but only as it has been for so many of my predecessors before me."

McIntyre's reaction could only be one of disbelief, but this was no more than Buchanan had expected.

"I have family papers, Doctor, though you might say that such papers are not proof, not of such an unlikely tale as mine. But I take it that you would believe quite independent evidence which, if you have not destroyed it, is to be found no farther than in your own records. Your father was doctor to both my father and my grandfather. He attended both of them at the times of their deaths. Go home, Dr McIntyre, and see for yourself whether I have spoken the truth."

....

I glanced at my clock. My account, though still unfinished, had already taken longer in the telling than I had expected and lunch would very soon be ready for us. For the first time since I had begun the story, Holmes interrupted me.

"I see you looking at the time, Watson. You've told the tale so well, my friend, that I'd be sorry should you attempt to hasten to finish it. That detail can wait for another time. It's already obvious what McIntyre found in his records. Had it been otherwise, there would be little point to the tale. Both Athol Buchanan's father and grandfather died at an age which was close to forty three years and two months."

I agreed.

"Then I can also assume," Holmes continued, "unless McIntyre is a man totally lacking in curiosity, that having confirmed that much of Buchanan's story, he would at least wish to have sight of the family papers to which Buchanan had also referred."

Again, I agreed.

"Then answer me just two questions, Watson. Buchanan spoke of the manner of his death being unpleasant – and his words were, 'as it has been for so many of my predecessors before me'. He implied that they had all died in a similar manner – of what?"

I hesitated. There did appear to be some clear similarity in the causes of death of Buchanan's father and grandfather. Earlier records, because of the state of medical knowledge at the time and the imprecise nature of diagnosis, made it less certain.

"Guess, Watson."

"Then I would have to say, a sudden wasting away of the lungs, what would be called a 'phthisis'. That is not a disease, merely a condition. It is usually caused by disease, like consumption, but the appearance of the condition is never sudden. Buchanan's father died within five days of its first appearance."

"And my last question. Since some if not all of the victims must have anticipated their demise, surely some must have taken steps to avert it."

"Oh! Yes," I answered. "Several. One locked himself away for two whole weeks before the time of his expected death, taking nothing but water from bottles which he had himself filled and sealed. He still died!"

"Enough, Watson!"

Holmes lay back in his chair, eyes half closed. The expression on his face was one I had seen before – something between ecstasy and excitement.

"Watson," he said, suddenly sitting up, "I suppose that I've waited almost twenty years for this day, since as a schoolboy I was accosted by a gypsy at St Giles Fair in Winchester. As the price of hearing 'a gypsy secret' I was persuaded into spending my last pennies on buying him a pint of ale, though I must say that the man did keep his word. He told me a strange story, a story so strange that it has never ceased to haunt my imagination – but perhaps no more!"

"I'm sorry," I said, "but I fear, Holmes, that you have completely lost me. I'm not even certain what we're talking about!"

"We are talking, Watson, about murder – four centuries of murder!"

Chapter Two

But a Moon Away

Upon that rather startlingly dramatic note, the discussion ended, for it was at that precise moment that Mary re-entered the room to say that lunch was now awaiting us on the table.

Once seated, Holmes did make a brief reference to the fact that I'd been acquainting him with what Mary had originally called "the odd business in Edinburgh". But, other than remarking that he'd found it a most fascinating story, he promptly turned the conversation to matters more commonplace.

Dearly as I would have wished to continue my earlier conversation with Holmes, there was no opportunity. For obvious reasons, Mary had prepared a more elaborate meal than we would usually have taken together, with the inevitable result that it took a deal more time in the eating than I had planned. Having now to complete both my morning and afternoon house calls, and return for evening surgery, I had to excuse myself from the table before the meal was finished. I left Holmes with Mary, committing myself to nothing more than the hope that Holmes would visit us again "in the not too distant future".

Already, I had the disturbing premonition that it might be a deal less distant than I could have wished. I had lived with Holmes for six years – long enough to know that once determined upon a course of action, Holmes was quite immovable in his resolution. I could recall no occasion in those six years when my strongest protestations against my involvement in one of Holmes' seemingly wilder or more dangerous schemes, had ever ended in anything other than my becoming, albeit still unwillingly, a full partner. I told myself that if Holmes did indeed have any such schemes, it would now be different. I no longer lived at Baker Street. I had a loyal wife to whom I had responsibilities, and a practice which demanded a duty to my patients.

And that was not all that exercised my mind on that afternoon. If I had understood Holmes correctly, then not only was he suggesting that Athol Buchanan was about to be murdered, but that each of his predecessors had suffered a similar fate – over a period of time which would, indeed, have had to cover four centuries. At first, I found the suggestion to be preposterous, yet was it any more unlikely than the explanation which I had hitherto assumed to be the true one?

McIntyre and I had, as yet, had little time to ex-change views upon the subject, but I felt certain that our thinking was similar. Remarkable though the story seemed, the only fact which was indis-putable was that Buchanan's father and grand-father had died at almost the exact same age, though not necessarily of precisely the same cause. The rest of the story hung entirely upon what was in the Buchanan family papers. They could be inaccurate. Certainly they were often vague and the language difficult. They could easily be read in a way, had perhaps even been written in a way, where "the wish was father to the thought". Yet now I could almost hear Holmes asking the question, "Why? Why would anyone go to the trouble of manufacturing such a legend, and of sustaining it over four centuries, when it would not appear to be to anyone's advantage. And is it certain that nothing in the Buchanan papers cannot be confirmed from some other, independent source?" I didn't know the answer to either of those questions!

Evening surgery was busy, though with fewer enquiries about the more gruesome details of the Whitechapel Murders. I arrived home with my mind now centred upon two things. I was tired and hungry. It was not until we had sat down to our evening meal that Mary said, "Sherlock wants you to go with him to Edinburgh."

That news was not entirely surprising.

"When?" I asked.

"Wednesday," was the reply.

"This Wednesday?"

"Yes. I assume so."

I started to laugh. I had half expected something of the sort, but not that Holmes should pay so little regard to the fact that circumstances had changed. I no longer lodged at 221B Baker Street, with little more to do than assist Mr Sherlock Holmes.

"Of course, you told him it was impossible."

"I didn't, John. I think you should go."

"But why, for Heaven's sake?"

"Because I know that you miss the excitement. You say that you don't, but I still see you reading all the crime reports in the newspapers. For weeks you've been talking about the Whitechapel Murders – and wondering whether Sherlock was involved. And then this business with James McIntyre. I've never seen you write such long letters. *I* can never persuade you to write anything longer than a prescription!"

I admitted that there was some truth in what Mary had said but, as to Holmes' suggestion, it was still quite impossible. And that was surely an end to the matter.

....

At a quarter to ten on the morning of Wednesday, October 3rd, I was waiting to meet Sherlock Holmes by the statue of George Stephenson, in the Great Hall of Euston Station. The intention was that we should board the express which left the departures platform at ten o'clock, bound for Birmingham, Carlisle, and Princes Street, Edinburgh.

Between the morning of Holmes' visit and now, nothing had happened which I could truthfully describe as totally unusual yet, if those events were taken together, it seemed quite impossible to believe that they were the result of nothing more than sheer coincidence!

Mary and I had not long finished our meal on Monday evening, when we were visited by Giles Anstruther and his sister Emmiline. There were three doctors with practices in the area around Paddington Station, myself, Anstruther and Jackson. Both, I regarded not merely as colleagues, but as friends. Both paid us the occasional unannounced visit, and not infrequently in the late evening when all of us were least committed by our work. Both men were bachelors, though Anstruther had a married sister, Emmiline, with whom Mary had formed a close friendship.

Emmiline had been visiting her brother that day and had accompanied him to our home that evening for a particular purpose. Emmiline had one child, a boy of eight years, but a frail and delicate child who had never enjoyed good health. Emmiline's husband was a lawyer of some means, owning both a fine town house and another on the Isle of Wight. For the sake of the child's health, both he and his mother spent the greater part of the winter away from the London fogs and in the cleaner, fresher air of Ventnor. Emmiline had, several times, suggested that Mary accompany them for a short holiday and, since they were about to leave London on Wednesday, she had come in a final effort to persuade Mary to go with them.

Mary had, hitherto, refused, Suddenly, it seemed, she much favoured the idea, explaining that she had been reluctant to leave me alone, but that now I too had the opportunity to take what might not be described as "a holiday", but an expedition which she was certain I would enjoy. She reminded me that I had remarked upon her looking a little pale of late and she was sure that some time away from the London fogs, to say nothing of these rather frightening murders, could do her nothing but good. Since she spoke only the truth, I had still to point out what I saw as an insurmountable obstacle to my going to Edinburgh – the welfare of my patients.

"How long," Anstruther enquired of me, "would you expect to stay in Edinburgh?"

I replied that since I still did not consider that to be a realistic possibility, I had given the matter no thought – though I supposed it could be at least a month.

"Then there's no problem," was the reply. "You know my practice is small. I could very easily accommodate your patients. If things become too busy, then Jackson will certainly be able to help out."

....

The circumstances which had brought me to Euston Station could therefore, be described as purely fortuitous. Yet my every instinct told that they were not, as surely as they told me that it was Sherlock Holmes who had somehow contrived them. I had resented those times at Baker Street when I knew that I had been manipulated. And that was my feeling now – a feeling heightened by the recollection that I had never yet found a counter to it. Having got his own way, Holmes would be at his most charming – the perfect companion, expansive, interesting, even witty! A ten-hour journey lay ahead of us, a journey during which Holmes might prove to be my only companion. If I were to show my disapproval by maintaining relative silence throughout that journey, then no-one would suffer but myself. Holmes would merely withdraw into some inner mental contemplation, a state that I had seen him maintain for periods of much longer than ten hours. I knew that I could but give in gracefully!

The journey began quietly enough, with both Holmes and myself reading the morning newspapers. I noted that Holmes still maintained his habit of confining his reading to the crime reports and the personal column of *The Times*, with the result that he finished his reading sooner than I and seemed anxious to enter into conversation.

"I assume," he said, "that your reading offers nothing new on the Whitechapel Murders, other than more speculation on this letter and postcard delivered to the Central News Agency."

It did not. The letter and postcard to which Holmes referred had both been signed, "Jack the Ripper" and purported to be written by the man responsible for the murders. The letter was received on Saturday morning, the postcard in the early hours of Monday morning. The speculation was upon whether they were genuine or merely some sick hoax. My own inclination was to think they were genuine.

"Why?" Holmes asked.

"Because," I replied, "the letter did seem to predict the two murders which occurred in the early hours of Sunday morning, and the postcard appears to contain knowledge not then known to the general public."

"Possibly, Watson, possibly. I've seen the letter – or rather a photograph of it. Don't look puzzled. I did tell you truthfully that I'd had no information from Scotland Yard. But I did have a visit from my brother Mycroft on Sunday evening. As you know, Watson, it seems that there is little which takes place in or around Whitehall to which Mycroft is not party. It was he who showed me the photograph."

"Then you must have formed some opinion."

"None, Watson – though I'll venture a suggestion. If *I* had reason to organise a series of brutal murders which I intended to have the appearance of being the work of one maniac killer, then I should probably feel it necessary to give my fictitious killer a name. In those albeit unlikely circumstances, I'm sure that I could think of no more appropriate name than 'Jack the Ripper'. You may be sure that it is one which will greatly capture the public imagination."

I was, naturally, attempting to work out the implications of what Holmes had said, but any question which I might have asked, was promptly anticipated.

"No, Watson. I will not be drawn further on the matter. I told you the last time I saw you that the investigation was in the hands of Chief Inspector Abbeline. And I should not be indulging myself in what is, I assure you, nothing more than idle speculation. In any event, my friend, we have a case of our own – and an unfinished story. This would seem to be a most appropriate time for you to finish it."

I could not help feeling some disappointment, and that all too familiar sense of uncertainty as to whether Holmes was speaking no more than the simple truth, or whether he did know something more than he was prepared to tell me. If it were the latter, then nothing I could say would change his mind – nor could I deny that I did have an unfinished story to tell.

....

Though I did finish my story, I do not intend to

record the detail of it here. It was no more than an account of the research which McIntyre had so far carried out upon the Buchanan family papers. Other than attempting to establish the most obvious facts, the ages at which various members of the family had died, the rest was concerned with attempts to establish the causes of death and with the measures taken by some in an attempt to avert the fatal consequences of the fulfilment of the curse. Some of those measures might be regarded as no less bizarre than the story itself, yet it was difficult to ignore the fact that all appeared to have been unsuccessful!

I avoid recording the detail here, partly because of its length, but mainly because it would establish nothing more than has already been established. Holmes asked surprisingly few questions of me but, apparently now satisfied that I had told him all I knew, he started upon what he described as, "the explanation which, Watson, is due, if not greatly overdue, to you".

"I said," he began, "that I'd waited twenty years for this case, and I referred to a youthful encounter with a gypsy at Winchester Fair. That man told me of a poison, known to his people since earliest times, a poison which could be given, but would show no effects for, he said, 'several weeks'. It would cause certain death, yet show no traces of its presence.

"My school, Winchester – I imagine much ahead of its time – had recently introduced science into its curriculum. The subject of chemistry already fascinated me, and I suppose it was that chance encounter at the fair which turned that interest in the special direction which you, Watson, know to be the subject of my greatest expertise – the chemistry of poisons."

"And is there such a poison?" I asked.

"I am certain, Watson, that there is – but I have not yet found it!" He held up his hand to silence my expected reaction. "Let me continue. The knowledge and use of poisons is as old as legend. Among the earliest 'poison lore' of the Asiatics are found repeated references to a poison which will slay long after its introduction. The gypsy at the fair described the poison as one 'known to his people since earliest times'. I'm sure you know, Watson, that the gypsies did *not* originate in Egypt. Pott's study of the gypsy language showed beyond any doubt that its origins lie in Sanskrit which is, of course, still a language of modern India. So the gypsies came from that same part of the world where the very first references are found to this unknown poison. In gypsy tradition the existence of such a substance has persisted down the centuries. It even has a name – *drab*.

"Unfortunately, it seems that name is now given to almost any poison. Go to any gypsy fair and, if you are persuasive enough, someone will sell you *drab*. I have analysed dozens of samples obtained in this way, but invariably they have been nothing other than well-known substances, from metallic poisons like arsenic and antimony to extracts of common plants or poisonous fungi such as the *death cap* or *fly agaric*."

"But," I said, "I don't see how any of this could have convinced you that this legendary poison is anything but that – legendary!"

"And you would be right, Watson. But there is upon my shelves at Baker Street a slim file, a file of eight cases collected painstakingly over many years. None of the cases is mine, but each is reliably documented. Each concerns an account of an unexplained death. Each death has certain facts in common. Each victim, though seemingly in good health, died suddenly from what you, Watson, have called a 'phthisis'. In each case, a post mortem failed to reveal any apparent cause of death. In each case, there was a possible suspect, but always a suspect able to prove themselves to be many miles away for some time before the victim's death."

"And you believe," I said, "that this will be the manner of Buchanan's murder, and that you can prevent it."

"I wish that I could be certain of that Watson. All of which I am certain is that we know the identity of the victim. We know the intended date of his death. We know how the murder will be accomplished, but neither the time nor the precise means. Don't expect too much of me, old friend. Buchanan is still alive, but it is possible that his murder has already been committed!"

....

As we had journeyed north, the carriage had become noticeably colder. With darkness now falling and the train still some miles short of Carlisle, I had pulled my coat about me and snuggled myself into the corner of the seat, hoping to retain what warmth my body might still provide. I had little thought of the possibility of sleep, but it seemed that the fatigue of the long journey was enough even to overcome the severe cold. I remember nothing more until Holmes shook me back into consciousness. The train had stopped. Through a heavily steamed carriage window, I could make out a painted sign lit by a row of flaring gas lamps and read the words, "Princes Street".

A steep flight of steps took us from the station platform up to street level, where an icy blast of wind suggested that we could have done no more than exchange the London fogs for the worse discomforts of some arctic clime. Holmes was clearly more intent upon the view. The black shape of Edinburgh Castle, standing high on its rock, rose dramatically before us, its outline sharply silhouetted against a cloudless, star-studded sky of deepest blue. Above it hung a moon in its third quarter. In seven days it would be full. What, I wondered, lay but one more full moon away – another triumph for Sherlock Holmes, or the death of Athol Buchanan?

Chapter Three

A Likely Suspect

On the day prior to our journey to Edinburgh, several things had been done on my behalf, all of them, I was assured, with my full knowledge and approval, though some of which seemed strangely absent from my recollection. One of these was that Holmes had taken it upon himself to telegraph McIntyre, informing him of our intended arrival and, of necessity briefly, explaining our purpose. McIntyre had sent a prompt reply, welcoming our visit and insisting that we be his guests.

Being, myself, a total stranger to Edinburgh, and having no more than an address, I had no reason to know anything either of McIntyre's circumstances, or even his whereabouts in the city. It was an omission soon to be remedied. The briefness of the carriage journey which took us from the railway station to his home, suggested

Edinburgh 1888

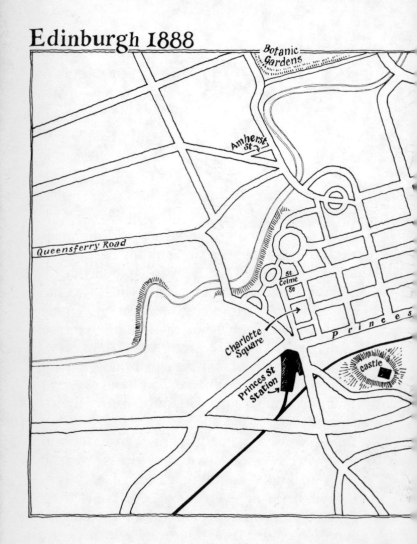

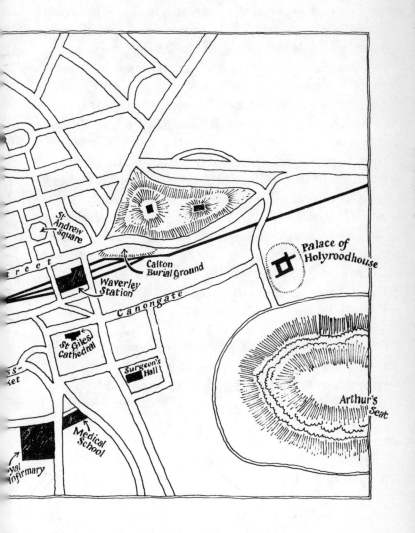

that it was in fact within ready walking distance. As to the house itself, even the moonlight was sufficient to reveal it as a residence of some elegance set upon one side of a spacious square with gardens at its centre. And if that first impression was favourable, then it was more than amply confirmed by the interior of the house – which was not merely large but bordering upon the opulent.

It was a matter upon which McIntyre was almost dismissive, assuring us that the credit for whatever degree of success he might appear to enjoy, must go to the ability and hard work of his father.

"Once you've established your practice at a sufficiently desirable address," he assured us, "then given a confident, yet kindly manner and a modicum of medical skill, it becomes difficult not to continue to prosper. It's one of life's injustices. But the fact remains that a sixpenny malady in the Portobello Road, is worth at least a guinea in Charlotte Square!"

I was grateful that the evening meal prepared for us was nothing like as sumptuous as our surroundings might have led us to expect. McIntyre had had the good sense to realise that Holmes and I would be tired, and more likely to enjoy the light repast which he had in fact provided. McIntyre did not, of course, know Holmes, who seemed always able to draw upon some vast reserve of nervous energy to sustain himself, almost without sleep, and for days upon end. Holmes did appear every bit as alert and energetic as he'd been when we'd met that morning at Euston Station.

In contrast, such was my own state of exhaustion that I fear I had nodded off more than once, even during the course of the meal. I felt indebted to McIntyre for his suggestion that I go to my bed. Holmes clearly had much to tell him, which he was sure I had already heard. What little new information that he, McIntyre, could add, could surely wait till morning.

I was asleep within an instant of my head touching the pillow and have no recollection of waking, even briefly, until it was to find the room brightly lit by shafts of sunlight through gaps around the still closed curtains. I looked at my watch. It was nine thirty.

The view from my room was all that last night's fleeting impressions might have promised. Charlotte Square was enclosed by four terraces of Georgian houses, that on the right broken by a small domed church clearly fashioned upon the design of St Paul's. The houses overlooked a circular, tree-planted garden with, at its centre, a memorial, which I was later to learn was to the late Prince Albert. Visible above the rooftops opposite, was the castle, not as dramatic in daylight as when I had first seen it last evening, but losing nothing in the sense of its domination over the whole city. It was a view which I could have enjoyed for much longer but for the lateness of the hour.

I began breakfast alone, McAlistair, the man-servant who tended to my needs, explaining that the "master" and Mr Holmes had breakfasted together at a little after eight. Dr McIntyre was still in morning surgery which he conducted in rooms in the basement at the back of the house, there being access for patients by way of the garden entrance in St Colme Street. Mr Holmes had gone out, promising to return by mid morning.

McIntyre joined me in the dining room as I was finishing a second cup of coffee. He had little to tell me, other than that he had visited Buchanan on the previous day to tell him of our visit.

"The man was clearly flattered at the interest being shown in him – especially by such a famous person as your colleague. The exploits of Mr Sherlock Holmes, 'the famous London detective' are, you may be surprised to know, followed with great interest, even this far from the metropolis! But I have to be honest with you, Watson, as I've been with Holmes. I suspect that Buchanan sees this as no more than a useful diversion to help him through the anguish of what he still sees as his last days."

"What was Holmes' reaction to that?" I asked.

"None, that I could detect," McIntyre replied. "The only thing in which he did show a deal of interest was the composition of the Buchanan household. That was an easy matter. Other than Buchanan, there is an elderly couple, the Campbells, who have been with him for many years. And there is a youth, Alexander, little more than a boy. Buchanan employed him six months ago to do the heavy work, carrying wood and coal, and water. They manage, though the house is slowly but surely falling down – and is not exactly clean!"

"And what are Holmes' immediate intentions?"

"I don't know Watson. There is nothing else I can recall that I should tell you, except perhaps that I do have one reservation about Holmes' whole theory –"

"Which is that you find it difficult to believe that simply in order to sustain a lasting belief in the 'curse' of some obscure sixteenth-century wise woman, generation after generation of her people have been prepared to commit murder." Holmes was standing in the room, having entered it without either McIntyre or myself having heard him.

"Well-oiled establishments have well-oiled doors," he said. "I told you last night, McIntyre, that your doubts lie in your inability to think other than with a western mind, though there are perhaps parallels even in western cultures. I might cite the ancient ritual of the vendetta, still to be found in today's Sicily. But why debate the point? If I succeed in my purpose, then you will have your proof enough! As to my immediate intentions, Watson, I really have no idea – but I will tell you that Edinburgh is a wonderful city, full of surprises! Walk along Princes Street and look across the Princes Street Gardens towards the castle, and suddenly you will see rapidly moving clouds of black and white smoke, rising, it would seem, from the gardens themselves. It is, of course, the railway, completely concealed, if not within tunnels, then in a deep cutting. I walked as far as the other station – which we would have reached had we travelled by the eastern route. Then, just beyond it, I boarded a tramcar to make the ascent to St Giles' Cathedral. The hill is too steep and the car too heavy for the two horses which pull it, but the difficulty is solved by a means as elegantly simple as it is undoubtedly picturesque. At the bottom of the hill, the car is met by a ragamuffin of a boy riding a horse. This he attaches to a shaft between the horses already harnessed to the car. Then he leads the equine trio and, to the accompaniment of much whip-cracking and shouting, and further aided by the clanging of the car bell and noisy encouragement of passengers, the ascent is accomplished. The boy promptly unhitches the horses and gallops down the hill to meet the next car. I found it most exhilarating!"

McIntyre, perhaps sharing my fear that Holmes was about to launch into a lengthy account of Edinburgh's more remarkable features, interrupted him.

"From which I guess that the purpose of your journey was not primarily to visit the Cathedral but, more likely, the University Medical School."

"Correctly, if not surprisingly, deduced. I did ask if you had a friend in the university through whom I might make a first approach. And I am obliged to you for your suggestion."

"Then you've met Dr Joseph Bell."

"Indeed I have, and arrangements have been made for my use of the medical school's chemical laboratories should I need them."

"And what did you think of Bell?"

"What should I think? Ah! You assume that he gave me a demonstration of what he obviously regards as his talent for deductive reasoning. Indeed he did."

McIntyre looked at Holmes in silence, obviously anticipating that he was to hear more.

"Then if it interests you," Holmes responded, "I found him with a group of medical students. Before I had the opportunity to introduce myself, he had described to them several of the things which I had in fact been doing this morning, before my arrival at the Medical School. They were relatively simple pieces of deduction, but quite well done."

"And?" I prompted.

"And I told him that he was completely wrong."

"Good heavens! Why?" McIntyre asked.

"I confess, he irritated me," Holmes answered. "The man's an exhibitionist and perhaps a little too self-opinionated. But worse, he has this infuriating habit of constantly describing his deductions as 'elementary' – which they are, though clearly the real intention is to create the quite opposite impression. But otherwise I found your Dr Bell to be tolerably pleasant and helpful. He did admit to having heard of my work and had the good grace to express his admiration of it."

"But to business," he continued, addressing himself to McIntyre. "I suppose that we should visit Buchanan. When do you suggest might prove convenient?"

....

The visit to the Buchanan house was arranged for that afternoon. Holmes excused himself, remarking that Edinburgh did have one serious shortcoming. It was unconscionably cold and windy. His intention was to go to his room and find some warmer clothing.

Hardly had he left us, when McIntyre burst into unaccountable laughter.

"I'm sorry, Watson," he said. "I am being most ill-mannered towards your friend, but I fear that I find the situation irresistably funny. But you're obviously not aware of the joke. I said that Holmes' reputation is well-known in Edinburgh. So, it happens, is that of Dr Joseph Bell – at least among the medical fraternity. There, you will find Bell's deductive powers are regarded as equal if not superior to those of Holmes – perhaps with no real justification other than Scottish pride. But I've known your friend long enough to see that the two men are really remarkably alike! My amusement is at Holmes' unfavourable reaction towards someone who might almost be himself!"

I'm sure that I fully shared McIntyre's amusement, whatever feelings of disloyalty might also have been in my mind. It was to be one of the few confidences which Holmes and I would not be sharing!

The Buchanan house must have been within no more than half a mile of Charlotte Square and close to the Botanic Gardens. The houses in Amherst Street were large, though any resemblance to McIntyre's rather splendid residence, ended there. Most of the properties were in a state of advanced dilapidation, number 47 being no exception. Built on four floors, if one included the attic rooms, not all of the windows were curtained, though the difference was made less obvious by an even accumulation of grime on the insides of the panes. The man who opened the door in response to our knocking, was reminiscent of some character from the works of Mr Dickens, yet he seemed not out of place in this setting. So bent was his back that it would have been difficult to gauge his true height. His clothing might once have been some kind of black uniform though stains of menus long past had merged into what was almost one unbroken shine. Long wisps of thinning white hair surrounded pale, drawn features and a pair of yellowing, myopic eyes observed us briefly before announcing, "Please to come in gentlemen. You are expected."

We were shown into a room which, whilst very large, was curiously oppressive. The walls appeared to be hung with some exceptionally dark paper though, in places where paintings had once been, there were patches of varying lighter shades, suggesting that the original colour might once have been a quite pleasant pink. And even if the heavy draperies had not at first matched, they did now, being much the same colour as the darkest of the paper. The room was grossly over-furnished, a fact made more obvious by the seeming lack of any two items which matched. On one wall was a massive fireplace of green marble. In it burned a smoking coal fire, the ashes of which spread completely across the hearth and onto a floor covered by a scattered assortment of rugs and carpets. At first completely hidden by a high backed chair pulled close to the fire, a figure rose slowly into view, lifting itself from the depths of the chair, then turning to face us, a hand outstretched in intended greeting.

Athol Buchanan was no less surprising than his house. Careless dressing, a shock of uncombed red hair and an unshaven face, totally failed to disguise a man who had about him a certain aristocratic air and who, in other circumstances, might well have graced the most elegant of social occasions. It was an impression confirmed by both the man's voice and manner. With introductions made, his first reference was to the room in which we stood.

"I might once have said that I live in a state of genteel poverty. I fear that it is no longer 'genteel'. I explained to Dr McIntyre that I have, long since, sold everything of value. It left the house so depleted of furnishing that it seemed easier to move everything that was left into this one room. And it is a great saving upon both light and fuel. I do have a bed, which is on the floor above us. And the servants' quarters remain untouched – they were fortunate in having nothing of value of which I was able to dispose.

"As to your presence here, gentlemen, particularly you, Mr Holmes, and you, Dr Watson. I can only repeat what I have already said to Dr McIntyre. I am both touched and honoured by your concern for my welfare, though I fear that your journey is wasted. Even your fabled skills, Mr Holmes, cannot change what is to be. But I would not want to appear either ungrateful or ungracious. I have been totally honest with you. If, knowing what I have said, it is still your wish to pursue the matter, then I am at your command."

"I would ask no more," Holmes answered. "Let me be equally honest in saying that I do not know that I can save your life. But I believe it is possible – as strongly as you do not. I shall ask little of you, and nothing which you might find unreasonable."

It had been obvious to me that we must visit the Buchanan house, but less so what was then to follow. Did Holmes envisage mounting some kind of guard over the man? Did he intend to keep some rigorous watch over everything that Buchanan might eat or drink? He had, as yet, given no hint of either, having asked only that we be allowed to explore the house and to meet the servants.

Campbell, we had already met, if briefly. Mrs Campbell, we found in the kitchen. She appeared several years younger than her husband and, if not sprightly, then still reasonably capable of her duties – which were, primarily, to cook. The boy, Alexander, we were told, was in the yard, chopping wood. Holmes' intention appeared to be no other than to introduce himself. As to the boy, he suggested to Campbell that he acquaint him of our presence. We wished to spend some little time in a careful examination of the house. He hoped that we might meet Alexander before leaving.

Buchanan had offered us a "conducted tour". Holmes expressed a preference that we be allowed the freedom to go where we wished. Buchanan had no objection and was certain that the servants would be equally agreeable. The house having perhaps fifteen or sixteen rooms, the task of making a "careful examination" might have been daunting, but for the fact that most of the rooms were empty. I was given the second floor. I was relieved to find that none of the rooms was occupied and, it seemed, all of them empty but for the very occasional small item of unused furniture. For that reason, I had soon reached the last room, with nothing in it but a chest of drawers. The first three drawers were empty. The fourth and last I had some difficulty in opening. It came away suddenly, eluding my grasp, and crashed to the floor. The noise brought Holmes, who cannot have been far away. He arrived in time to find me staring, I suppose rather stupidly, at something lodged in the corner of the drawer which now lay by my feet.

"I'm sorry," I said. "It was the unexpectedness of it. I was sure it was a dead rat or some grey, furry creature. I see now that it's no more than the remains of something very mouldy, possibly bread. And that's all I've found, Holmes. It might have helped if you'd told us what we were looking for."

"We aren't looking for anything," Holmes replied. "We're just looking as though we were looking."

He'd stepped over to the window which looked down into the yard.

"Here, Watson. Take a look. Tell me what you think."

In the yard was a youth chopping firewood. I could see that he had black curly hair, but little else – until he stood up. He was short and stocky, and his skin was unusually dark. "Holmes!" I said. "The boy could be a gypsy!"

"One cannot be certain, Watson. Like London, Edinburgh is a seaport. There must be many foreigners here – but you are probably right. I think that we now have one more piece to the puzzle – a victim, a date, a motive, a method, and now a likely suspect!"

"But, Holmes!" I said. "If you're right, then you cannot simply leave it at that. We must do something!"

"And we shall," was the reply. "We shall return to McIntyre's, and we shall wait. We could wait here, but McIntyre's heating is so much better."

Chapter Four

An Odd Unearthing

Some ten days had passed since our visit to the Buchanan house, and during that time, we had not once returned. Holmes had said simply that we should "wait". Not unnaturally, I'd asked him, "For what?" I have earlier remarked that it was not always possible to tell whether Holmes' replies were merely truthful or deliberately evasive. This was surely another case in point. "I don't know," was his answer, though he'd added, "I may know when it happens."

It was Holmes himself who had listed as the pieces of the puzzle already in his possession, "a victim, a date, a motive, a method, and now a likely suspect". I could only assume that he was waiting for the suspect to make some move, though I could not see how he was to know this when the suspect was at 47 Amherst Street and we were at Charlotte Square! For whatever reasons, it was not a matter that appeared to be causing Holmes the least concern. Indeed, anyone not acquainted with the true reasons for our presence in Edinburgh, could have been forgiven for assuming that it was for no other purpose than a holiday!

The weather being cold but fine, it afforded ample opportunity for exploration of what is undeniably a fine and interesting city. In other circumstances, it was an experience which I could have enjoyed. In fact, I found it to be something of an embarrassment. Not only did I feel that we were abusing McIntyre's very generous hospitality, but I was constantly reminded of the situation when writing my frequent letters to Mary – not with any news of progress on the case, but rather relating some trifling item like having watched the Royal Scots Guard parading in Princes Street, or having visited a coffee shop in St Andrew Square, where a blind beggar sat outside, "reading" aloud from the Bible, his finger seemingly tracing each line, though it was said he had never been seen to turn the page! Holmes had, admittedly, paid several visits to the Advocates' Library by St Giles, the Library of the University and Register House in Princes Street – the equivalent of London's Public Records Office. His stated purpose was to seek independent confirmation of some items in the Buchanan family papers which, following our visit, he had brought back with him to Charlotte Square. But if he'd had any success, he had not confided in me.

I can only assume that it was a growing sense of impatience and frustration at Holmes' apparent inactivity and lack of concern, that set my mind upon a course which I cannot now recall without feeling some sense of shame. They were thoughts which at first I rejected as unworthy, yet as the days had passed I had become convinced that they were no more than the unpalatable truth. Several times, I had been on the point of confronting Holmes with what was on my mind, but each time had pulled back from the brink – of accusing my old friend of a degree of unmitigated ruthlessness that I still found difficult to believe possible of him.

We had spent yet another day doing nothing more than sightseeing. We had climbed that afternoon to Arthur's Seat, the highest point on a hill that stood on the eastern side of the city and which afforded magnificent views, not only of the city itself, but south to the Pentland Hills and north to the long sweeping stretch of coastline which formed the Firth of Forth. Even the great castle of Edinburgh seemed dwarfed beneath us.

The walk had been tiring, but had done much for our appetites. Even Holmes, never an enthusiastic eater, had done more than justice that evening to a most flavoursome piece of Scottish sirloin. Almost at the end of dinner, McIntyre had been called out to some emergency, leaving Holmes and myself to retire to the smoke room to enjoy yet another bottle of our host's most excellent port wine. Holmes, preferring his pipe to McIntyre's fine Havana cigars, had settled himself by the fire, his whole attitude and expression suggesting that he had, at that moment, nothing of any great consequence upon his mind. It came therefore as even more of a surprise that he should suddenly address me in the manner that he did.

"Watson, I could hardly be unaware that for several days past, I have been the subject of your silent yet increasing disapproval. I believe that I am very well aware of the reasons for it, yet I find myself disappointed."

"If you know the reasons, Holmes, then I see no cause for you to feel disappointed," I retorted, perhaps in a tone that was a little too obviously defensive.

"The disappointment," Holmes answered, "is only that you have not chosen to confront me with the things of which you so clearly disapprove."

Holmes had now quite deliberately placed me in a corner. Perhaps because of the length of my absence from Baker Street, I had become more resentful of being constantly manipulated by Sherlock Holmes. I had still not forgotten the very strange sequence of apparent "coincidences" which had brought me to Edinburgh in the first place. If Holmes wanted to know what was in my mind, then he should! The disadvantage would surely be his!

"You believe that Athol Buchanan is about to be murdered. You believe this youth, Alexander, to be the murderer. The method of Buchanan's murder will be to administer secretly an unknown poison, a poison which will show no effects for some considerable period of time. The manner of Buchanan's death will be a sudden, short lived and fatal phthisis. Between the time of administering the poison and the onset of the fatal symptoms, the murderer will leave the Buchanan house. In the event of his being apprehended, he will be able to show that he has been many miles from that place since the time of his leaving. No trace of any poison will be found in Buchanan's body."

"A pessimistic, but not impossible prediction," Holmes interjected. "But continue, Watson."

"Since no-one is watching either Buchanan or this youth, there is only one possible event of which you can become aware – that Alexander has left. That can mean only one thing. The poison has already been administered. Is it Buchanan's life that really interests you, Holmes, or is it only the poison? For now, you will indeed have your poison – inside the man! Your first visit when we arrived in Edinburgh was to the medical school laboratory. Perhaps, with a sample of the man's blood which you know to contain the poison, you can identify it, even find an antidote. The first I see as realistic – given time. But what of the second, or do you think that is of lesser importance?"

Holmes had neither moved nor even changed his expression.

"I had assumed, Watson, that that was exactly your thinking. The fault is mine. On the basis of what you know, it is the only obvious conclusion which you could have drawn. Indeed, what you describe, could happen. If it did, I should consider that I had failed. I still do not put my chances of success as high – though I have done rather more than you are aware of.

"First, let me say this. You wonder why I've not taken the obvious precautions, like mounting some kind of close watch upon both Buchanan and the boy. In the past, others have taken some extraordinarily elaborate precautions. All have failed. Consider, Watson, exactly what we might mean when we speak of an 'unknown poison'. It might be a powder, a liquid, even a vapour. And in how many ways might it be administered? By mouth, by being inhaled, through contact with the skin, a scratch, a sharp object tipped with the poison. I believe the possibilities to be too numerous to counter. Instead, I have chosen to pursue a course of action which involves enormous risk. But I do it with Buchanan's full knowledge and consent."

Whilst McIntyre and I had imagined that we were assisting Holmes in searching the Buchanan house, Holmes had been using the time mainly to provide himself with an opportunity to engage in private conversation with Buchanan. Having glimpsed the youth, Alexander in the yard, during the brief time we had visited Mrs Campbell in the kitchen, he had sought first to establish the precise circumstance of the boy's employment in the house. It appeared that "Duncan", Alexander's predecessor had quite suddenly, and inexplicably, "left". Alexander had appeared upon the very day following, offering his services. Buchanan had seen it as no more than fortuitous. Holmes saw it differently. Taken together with the boy's appearance, he was at least satisfied that it provided him with a likely suspect. Buchanan had offered to dismiss the youth. Holmes had demurred. If this were indeed the murderer, then it was better that his movements should be known.

"You will remember, Watson, that in the house, you suggested that it might have helped if I'd told you what you were looking for."

"And you replied that we weren't looking for anything."

"I also said that we were just looking as though we were looking – or rather you and McIntyre were. Buchanan and I were talking, but in a place where we could observe the youth in the yard. As I'd asked, Campbell went out to tell him of our presence in the house, and what we were doing. If you, Watson had hidden something incriminating in or around the house, and had just been told that someone was about to –"

There was no need for Holmes to finish. I would, of course be anxious to ensure that whatever I'd hidden remained undiscovered. Yet, obviously the youth had merely continued to chop wood in the yard.

"So," Holmes continued, "the poison was not yet in the house. It had, therefore, either still to be fetched, or to be delivered. It is that event which I hope to discover."

Holmes paused. It did not require any lengthy contemplation to realise that what he was suggesting could be extremely difficult, if not impossible. There could be many callers at the house. The boy might go out frequently, and for many reasons.

"There was a moment when I too thought it might be near impossible. One thing convinced me otherwise – and in these last few days I've established a piece of knowledge which could be of further help. I've been able to confirm a surprising amount of what appears in the Buchanan papers, though only one thing which might be of use. Taken together with those papers which I said reside in my file at Baker Street, I'm confident that I can predict the time at which the poison must be administered – to within three days. But there is one more important thing. We have spoken many times of this 'unknown poison', a substance clearly remarkable in the lapse of time before its effects appear, in the manner in which it kills, in the absence of any traces of it in the victim.

Yet, Watson, there is about it something still more remarkable – the fact that its identity has remained a secret for hundreds, perhaps thousands, of years. There can be only one explanation. Its secret has been known to but a very few, and those who have known that secret have guarded it with a zealousness which must mean that it has something about it of an almost religious significance.

"Translate that into practicalities and it must be used only in a way designed to minimise its accidental discovery. Of course it would not be kept in the house. Nor will it be delivered. That method is clearly fraught with dangers. It must be fetched. And it must be fetched at a fairly precise time – as close as is possible to the time of its intended use."

All that I saw, but not how it got us any nearer to knowing that "precise time".

"That, Watson, is simple. Alexander has his half days off, but they are often irregular. If old Campbell's back should be proving unusually troublesome, then any outings planned by Alexander may be cancelled at very short notice. Let me add that since our visit, Campbell has been having remarkably frequent trouble with his back! So, if the boy wishes to leave the house for the purpose I've suggested, what do you imagine that he'll do, Watson:"

"I suppose, make it appear to be a matter of some importance, invent some good story – certainly give good advance warning of his intended expedition."

"Brilliant, Watson. That's exactly what he must do – and that's the news for which I've been waiting."

It sounded convincing as Holmes had told it but, as I thought more of it, I realised that it was almost entirely supposition and guesswork, I might have said, even rather wild guesswork. I was not at all convinced that it would work, though I had much rather Holmes had told me what was in his mind, than allow me to think the thoughts of which I now felt so deeply ashamed.

"You are right, Watson, though I would prefer not to think of any of it as "wild". I said that it involved enormous risk. And if it fails, Watson, then we will have left only those last desperate measures which you yourself suggested. You ask why I did not tell you. You have just answered your question. I decided that I preferred your silent disapproval to what I am sure would have been your growingly vociferous expression of what are now your obvious doubts. But let us not quarrel, my friend. There is a question which I have been meaning to ask you."

....

When McIntyre returned, Holmes had taken out all of the Buchanan papers, including those records which had belonged to McIntyre's father at the times he had attended the deaths of both Buchanan's father and grandfather. It was the few notes which referred to Buchanan's grandfather which Holmes had handed to me.

"I'm afraid they're very sparse," McIntyre said, "and hardly readable. I should explain that my father had just qualified and it was his first position – acting as a locum for a Dr Thomas."

"It isn't that," Holmes interrupted. "It's this curious pencilled addition, presumably added at some later time, just 'B and H', ringed with a large question mark."

"I can think of nothing," McIntyre said. "'B' could obviously be for Buchanan, but as to the 'H' . . . I don't think it's medical shorthand. Perhaps something to do with some subsequent event, some item of news . . ."

"Then," I said, "I'm not likely to be of help. Until I came here, if anyone had asked me anything of Edinburgh, about all I knew was that it was the capital of Scotland, had a castle – and, of course, I'd heard of Burke and Hare, the notorious body-snatchers!"

"It's hardly likely to be Burke and Hare," McIntyre retorted, "though the date's about right."

"Remind me of Burke and Hare," Holmes asked.

"Little to tell," McIntyre answered. "They were not, in fact, body-snatchers. They did supply bodies, sixteen in all, at prices varying from £7.10s to £14, to a Dr Knox of Surgeon's Square. But they didn't dig them up. They murdered them. Unfortunately, since the bodies were used by Dr Knox for public demonstrations of anatomy, some of the victims were recognised! Hare turned 'King's Evidence'. Burke was hanged. You can still see his skeleton in the anatomical museum at the university. I don't see that any of that helps. The Burke and Hare murders were in 1828. Buchanan's grandfather died in the January of that year. But that would seem to be the only connection. If you're interested, Holmes, I'm sure that I still have one of my father's books, which is the full account of the trial."

Holmes *was* interested. McIntyre and I left him reading it when we went to bed.

....

Despite my efforts to be otherwise, I always seemed to be last to arrive at the breakfast table. The morning of the following day was no exception – except that on my entering the dining-room, I was urged by McIntyre to make my selection from the sideboard as quickly as possible. "The kedgeree is particularly good. The cold beef is what you sampled last night, though the ham is also quite excellent. I know that you and Holmes are amazingly frugal in your eating habits at breakfast, but I suggest that this morning, Watson, you indulge yourself – shamelessly. Holmes has something to tell us which he assures me will capture our imagination. Since he still stubbornly refuses to take anything but his toast, marmalade and coffee, I suggest that you and I, Watson,

AUTHENTIC

CONFESSIONS

OF

WILLIAM BURK,

Who was Executed at Edinburgh, on 28th January
1829, for Murder, emited before the Sheriff-
Substitute of Edinburgh, the Rev. Mr Reid,
Catholic Priest, and others, in the Jail, on 3d
and 22d January.

EDINBURGH :

Printed and Sold by R. Menzies, Lawnmarket.

———

1829.

Price Twopence.

enjoy this promised mental stimulation to the accompaniment of its gastric counterpart. In any event, you'll find that a good lining on the stomach is most effective against the cold. I'm told that there was snow last night on the Pentlands."

Holmes began by assuring us that what he had to tell appeared to shed no new light upon the Buchanan case, but he was certain that he had solved the mystery of the pencilled addition made by McIntyre's father. He had, as we knew, stayed from his bed on the previous evening to read the book which gave an account of the trial of Burke and Hare. What neither he, nor indeed McIntyre had suspected was that the book also contained, within the pocket often provided for notes, and forming a part of the back cover, a number of cuttings from the *Caledonian Mercury* of the time, and a pamphlet allegedly containing confessions of William Burke (spelled Burk) given before the Sherrif-Substitute and a Catholic priest, a week before his execution.

Burke and Hare, originally Irish labourers lived in Edinburgh, in Tanner's Close. Their income was derived from two disreputable lodging houses, in which business they were assisted by two women, Nell Macdougal and Maggie Laird.

"In August 1828," Holmes continued, "a soldier, lodging at Burke's, had collided with Burke and Hare as they were carrying down the stairs, a tea-chest containing the body of a woman. The lid of the tea-chest had come loose. Both Burke and

Hare were certain that the soldier had seen nothing, but Nell Macdougal, who'd witnessed the incident was uncertain – uncertain enough to insist that no more murders were committed until they could be sure that nothing had been reported to the police. Hare was readily agreeable, Burke less so. Burke spent much of his time drinking and, within a day, he'd run out of money to buy more. That very morning, as he'd passed the Calton Burial Ground, he'd witnessed a funeral. 'And it wasn't,' he'd said, 'one of these graves with the spiked railings around it!'."

Against his better judgement, Hare was persuaded to accompany Burke to the Calton Burial Ground, that night. "Now here," Holmes said, "comes the first clue to the mystery, and I'm now quoting from Hare, according to the *Caledonian Mercury*."

Willie was still very drunk. I don't know where he'd got the money. He said he knew where the grave was, but was a long time in finding it. I told him he was wrong. You could see it wasn't new. But he says I'm a stupid . . ., and lifts his shovel at me. He says the man buried that morning was Stuart Buchanan, and that's the name on the grave. I could have told him that if the man was buried that morning, they wouldn't have put up a headstone – not that soon. But I says nothing, cause he'd have probably killed me.

We digs in turn while the other holds the light. Burke gets to the coffin first and prises off the lid. What's inside, I wouldn't never have believed. I hear about hair that goes on growing after death – but not like this. The coffin's full of it. It gives me a bit of a turn. Burke, he just walks off, and leaves me to put the earth back best I could.

"The cutting is ringed in pencil, and with a question mark, Your father, McIntyre, was simply asking the obvious question. Did Burke and Hare accidentally dig up Buchanan's grandfather's grave. It answers one question, but instantly raises another!"

"The hair," McIntyre said, speaking my own thought aloud.

"Surely hair does not grow after death," Holmes remarked.

McIntyre and I agreed. It is a commonly held belief. The shrinking of the skin may give it the slight appearance of growing – but nothing more.

"Perhaps it is of no matter," Holmes said, "but I find myself curious to know what Hare did see."

"That," McIntyre answered, "you'll never know. Even if you'd any thoughts of playing resurrectionist yourself, the Calton Burial Ground has been closed and abandoned these many years."

The conversation was interrupted by the appearance of McAlistair. "A note," he said, "for Mr Holmes, from a Mr Buchanan. The boy who brought it said that it was urgent."

Chapter Five

A Night of Vigil

At a few minutes before midnight on Thursday, October 18th, Sherlock Holmes and I boarded a carriage in Charlotte Square – our destination, Amherst Street. The note from Buchanan, which had interrupted our breakfast, had arrived two days earlier. In those two days Holmes had been gone from the house on several occasions, but saying only that they were small matters to which he needed to attend. Still feeling not a little foolish and ashamed about my recent outburst, I was possibly more reluctant than usual to press him for further information.

What I did know was that Holmes had, yet again, achieved the seemingly impossible. What I had very inadvisedly described as his "wild gues-ses" now looked to be quite remarkably accurate predictions. Buchanan's note was to say that Alexander had made a special plea that he be allowed, as was his normal entitlement, to take off the afternoon of Thursday, October 18th. The reason which he had given was that he wished to visit the Forth Railway Bridge to witness what promised to be a delicate, though spectacular, engineering operation on the first of the three now partially constructed cantilevers.

Railway bridges to cross the estuaries of both the Forth and Tay had been begun in 1882. The Tay Bridge had been completed in the previous year, 1887. Though the Forth Bridge was not due for completion until 1890, it was already in an advanced state of construction and providing the population of Edinburgh with a popular sight-seeing attraction. Though Holmes and I had glimpsed a distant view of the bridge from Arthur's Seat, for a close inspection it was necessary to travel to Queensferry, the seaport on the Forth, some eight or nine miles west of the centre of the city.

Buchanan's note, I suspect at Holmes' suggestion, had also contained the opportunity to reply without arousing any suspicion. The boy who had delivered it had been used in the past to summon McIntyre and, since the child could neither read nor write, there was no danger of his discovering its contents. McIntyre had, in fact, delivered Holmes' reply on the following day – on the pretext of giving medical attention to Mrs Campbell. Since that letter was sealed, McIntyre knew no more of its contents than I.

....

The carriage took us only to the end of Amherst Street, the intention being that Holmes did not wish to draw attention to our arrival at the Buchanan house. It was but a short walk, for which I was grateful, the night being extremely cold and the pavements quite icy. The houses in Amherst Street, as seemed commonplace in Edinburgh, had a ground floor built at some higher level above the pavement than would normally be seen in London. The consequence of that was that while shortening the steps to the basement entrance, it also required a considerable flight of steps to reach the main door. This had not struck me as having any particular disadvantage, until I discovered that it was not our intention to enter number 47 by the door, but instead, through one of the ground floor windows!

The purpose of this hazardous operation did not become clear for several moments. Having quietly closed the window behind us, Buchanan, whose voice I had recognised, closed the curtains, and only then lit a lamp. We were in the large, oddly furnished room to which we had been shown on our first visit.

"You have carried out my instructions exactly?" Holmes asked.

Buchanan assured him that he had.

"Alexander left at midday, accepting a ride part way on the coal cart, as you predicted he would. So we do know that he was at least going in the direction of Queensferry. He returned shortly after darkness. As you instructed, Holmes, I have had nothing to eat nor to drink since the boy's return – and I have had no contact with him. I sent the Campbells to bed at ten. At eleven, I made much noise going to my own room – which is above this, then crept back down the stairs to this room, locking the door behind me. Alexander and the Campbells are, to the best of my knowledge, in their beds. They believe that I am, also."

"Excellent!" was Holmes' response. "And now we wait. Ask me not, for what. From this point we play the game in whatever way events may determine. Tell me, how easily can sounds from this room be heard in the rest of the house?"

"Hardly at all. If we were to make some loud noise or raise our voices – then perhaps. The reverse is not true. As you have seen, gentlemen, the rest of the house is largely devoid of carpets, and most of the boards creak. We will hear anyone who moves in the rest of the house. You will see that I have laid in a good stock of coal. Our vigil will at least be warm."

Once settled comfortably before a warm fire, conversation came easily enough. Holmes took the opportunity to tell Buchanan of his odd discovery of the possible connection between Buchanan's grandfather and the murderers, Burke and Hare. I imagined that he had hoped that Buchanan might confirm that his grandfather was, in fact, buried in the Calton Burial Ground.

That much he could confirm, though not that the grave disturbed by Burke and Hare was, for certain, that of his grandfather.

"You know that Buchanan is a common name in Edinburgh. And it seems that in the early part of the century, Stuart was popular as a Christian name. I'm sure that my father told me that there were no less than five Stuart Buchanans buried in that same place. But I *can* tell you why the burial ground was closed – and even that was, I suppose, because of a most unlikely circumstance."

"There are, in some parts of the city, outcrops of a rock which is called *oil shale*. It is, as the name implies, shale which is impregnated with natural oil. Such an outcrop exists on the rising land above the Calton Burial Ground. Some time in the early twenties, there was new building work being carried out in that area, in the course of which, a spring was discovered. If that provided any cause for concern, it was short lived. Within days of its discovery, it had vanished – obviously having found some new underground route. What no-one had realised was that the spring was now running through cracks in the oil shale and carrying an unpleasant mixture of oil and water into the burial ground. The effects did not become apparent for several years. Stories told by gravediggers of earth, even coffins, saturated in oil were conveniently dismissed. It was not until everything from the grass to the trees began slowly to die off, that the problem had to be recognised.

Attempts to find and divert the spring and even to replant the burial ground all failed. It was closed. All that has been done is to erect a high wall around it to hide the dereliction. But it is like the rest of your story, Mr Holmes. It would seem to have no connection with our present concerns."

Holmes agreed. By way of refreshment, Holmes had brought with him some bottles containing claret and water. That, the warm fire and lively conversation, helped pass the first few hours pleasantly enough. But it was not to last. We had, perhaps, been too generous with the coal and, having realised a need to be more economical, I certainly had begun to feel the cold. Conversation also ran out. We had sat in near silence for a half hour when I noticed that Buchanan was asleep. The time was now but a little after five o'clock. Another hour passed and still nothing unusual had happened. Determined though I was, not to sleep, I found my eyes frequently closing. I was becoming certain that I could not sustain my resolution to stay awake for very much longer, when I saw that Holmes was looking towards the ceiling. I too became slowly aware of faint sounds, though not I thought from directly above us. I looked at my watch. It was six thirty – perhaps time for the servants to be stirring. I asked if we should wake Buchanan, who was still sleeping soundly. Holmes thought not yet – it was best that we stayed where we were, at least for a little longer.

The fire was almost out and the coal exhausted. The room was cold. My feelings were of mixed excitement and impatience. My mind was alert to every sound, and there was no longer the least danger of my falling asleep! For several minutes there had been noises below us, from what I took to be the kitchens. It was now approaching seven thirty. Almost at the instant that the hands off my watch reached the half hour, there was a resounding crash. The echoes of it had hardly faded before it was followed by a half strangled cry. I would have described it as a cry, almost of anguish!

....

Buchanan was awake and sitting bolt upright in his chair. Holmes and I were on our feet, I clutching in my hand my old army revolver, which I'd brought with me in my jacket pocket.

"I don't think you'll need the gun, Watson," Holmes said. He turned to Buchanan. "I'm sorry, but I want you to remain here. Let Watson and myself out by the door and lock it behind us. Open it to no-one but Watson or myself."

I followed Holmes into the hallway and down the stairs to the kitchens. By an open door, we could see the unmistakable figure of Campbell, standing with his back to us, and not moving. Even as we got closer, he remained, it seemed transfixed, so that we had to push past him into the room.

All that was immediately apparent was that a chinaware jug and basin, of the kind used in any bedroom, had fallen from a wooden table to the floor. The china lay in a thousand pieces, while a large pool of water was beginning to drain away through the cracks in the stone floor. Campbell had suddenly found his tongue!

"It's not possible! I left it standing well on the table. It couldn't have fallen off!"

"It didn't fall off – just as I'm sure that the door to the yard didn't leave itself open to let the freezing air in. Just tell me, where would the jug and basin have been taken?"

"To Mr Buchanan's bedroom, though I'd yet to add some hot water from the kettle. He likes the chill off it, you see."

"Yes. Yes. And what does he use it for? Tell me – exactly."

"Well – you know what he'd use it –"

Holmes took the man's arm and shook him, I thought quite roughly.

"Concentrate man! Answer my question! What does he use it for? What does he do with it first?"

Campbell had begun to shake.

"Does Mr Buchanan perhaps use it first to rinse his mouth?" I asked.

"Yes," came the answer. "And then he washes . . ."

Holmes had let go his arm.

"Never mind. See if you can find Alexander. I'm sure you won't – but go and look. Then you and Mrs Campbell are to stay out of this room. Watson – you've got your medical bag."

"In the room where –"

"Get it, quickly, Watson. I need an eye dropper and some sort of bottle."

....

When I returned with the bottle and dropper, Holmes was on his knees and crawling around with his magnifying glass. He was clearly excited.

"We've got it, Watson! It's all here – if we can read all of it! But this much I do know – the boy has tried and failed! And we have the poison, or we will have it if you give me that dropper and the bottle before everything goes down the cracks in the floor or evaporates. And now you'll need paper and pencil. Touch nothing, but draw me a sketch of everything you can see. And I could have some items for you to add to it when you're finished."

"Buchanan's still in the room," I said. "Can I tell him he's safe?"

"He can come down here but, 'No', Watson. You most certainly cannot tell him that he's safe!"

Watson's Sketch

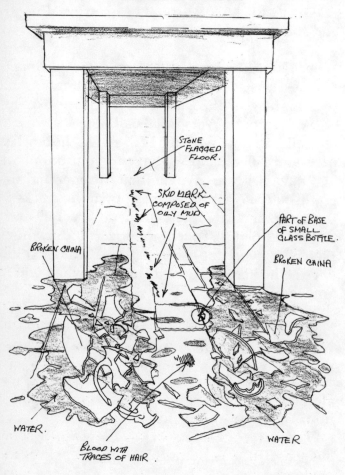

STONE FLAGGED FLOOR.

SKID MARK COMPOSED OF OILY MUD.

PART OF BASE OF SMALL GLASS BOTTLE.

BROKEN CHINA

BROKEN CHINA

WATER.

WATER

BLOOD WITH TRACES OF HAIR.

Chapter Six

The Last Victim

Much happened in the next two hours. Using the eye dropper with which I had provided him, Holmes set about saving as much of the water that had spilled onto the floor as was possible. It filled not only the bottle which I had given him, but the better part of a second. He seemed well pleased at that.

I, meanwhile, made my sketch, whilst Buchanan, who had joined us, stood watching in silence. Holmes, having been on his knees for a good half hour, at last rose stiffly to his feet.

"I'm sorry," he said, "if I have kept you in some suspense. It was necessary – before any of the evidence was lost. The story it tells would appear to be a relatively simple one. Alexander did, indeed, return last evening with a quantity of poison contained in a small glass bottle. This morning, while Campbell had gone into the next room to fetch a kettle of boiling water, he attempted to introduce it into the jug, already part filled with cold water. That jug, Buchanan, would have been taken to your bedroom where, in the normal course of events, your first act would have been to use some of the water to rinse out your mouth. That act would have proved fatal!

"What it is impossible to know, is whether or not the poison was, in fact, introduced. All that we do know is that at or about that point, the youth slipped, either upon something which was already on the floor, or on something that was on the heel of one of his boots. Essentially, it is mud, but mud mixed with oil or grease of some kind. I have enough of it to examine, but that must wait. The marks on the floor tell us that he slid under the table and, that in so doing, he perhaps grasped at the table, but succeeded only in pulling down the jug and basin on top of him. He also struck the back of his head on the floor. There is a distinct smear of blood and hair. *And*, he dropped the bottle which still contained, or had contained, the poison.

"I have found one corner of the base of the poison bottle. That tells me the bottle's shape and size, the fact that it contained a liquid and not a powder – but most importantly, that the poison is on the floor – whether or not he had succeeded in pouring it into the jug! Some of it is now most certainly in the two bottles which I have filled."

"But why," I asked, "did the boy then leave so

suddenly? He could merely have said that he'd slipped and pulled over the jug and basin."

"There are several possible reasons," Holmes answered. "My guess would be panic. His first instinct was to pick up the 'evidence' in the shape of the pieces of the broken poison bottle, and leave before anyone could stop him."

"If that is so," I suggested, "then surely it's over, at least so far as any danger to Buchanan is concerned. But you said, Holmes. . ."

"That it wasn't over. And it isn't Watson. Alexander has to try again. And if my deductions are correct, and if he's to appear to fulfil the curse, he has only forty-eight hours left in which to do it. I said the poison must have near religious significance. The act of administering it must also be surrounded by that same sense of 'mission' – all it something resembling a religious fervour. I'm certain that the boy will see it in no other way. Therefore, he must succeed! He must return here, to try again, no matter what risks he may now see in doing so."

....

By ten o'clock that same morning, arrangements had been made for Buchanan to pack a bag and go to McIntyre's house. There he was to stay, it was expected for no more than the next two days. Holmes had taken the bottles and was on his way to the chemical laboratories of the University Medical School. I was still at Amherst Street, as were Campbell and his wife. The kitchen floor had been cleared, in strict accordance with careful instructions left by Holmes, and which I had supervised.

Two men, a Mr Lightfoot and a Mr McCrae, of the Canongate Private Detective Agency, had just arrived at the house. Apparently, Holmes had contacted that establishment two days previously. I thought that an odd circumstance, but it was not one that I was about to question. The reason for their presence was simple. If Alexander were to return, they were to confiscate anything he might be carrying, hold him and call the police. Alexander would be accused of theft – no more than a convenient invention until Holmes had finished his work. The charge would then be changed to one of "attempted murder". If Alexander had not returned by six that evening, Messrs Lightfoot and McCrae would be replaced by two others – and so on, every eight hours, until the task was accomplished. I was now free to return to Charlotte Square.

....

Holmes was gone all day. Buchanan retired to his bedroom at nine. I had snatched some sleep that afternoon but, by eleven, was beginning again to feel the effects of a night without sleep. At eleven fifteen, McIntyre went to his bed, suggesting that I did the same. I was about to act on that suggestion, when Holmes returned, looking impossibly fresh and alert, but I thought troubled.

"Troubled, Watson?" he said. "No. I think not.

'Frustrated', or perhaps, 'impatient' might be better words, though I have no just reason to feel either. As you may have gathered, Watson, I have so far failed to identify the poison, even to isolate it. But I had no reason to suppose that it would be anything but difficult. Has Alexander returned?"

"No," I answered. "That is, not to my knowledge. There's certainly not been any message delivered here."

"There would have been if he had. I had not thought that he would leave it so long."

Troubled, frustrated, impatient – whatever the true cause of the unease which Holmes had shown on his return, I sensed that the news of Alexander's failure to appear was disturbing him rather more. But I had no opportunity to question him upon it.

"You must forgive me, Watson. I appreciate your kindness in waiting up for me until this late hour, when I know that you must yourself be tired, but I think that I too must go to my bed. Perhaps, old friend, you can find something to relax me and ensure a few hours' sleep – but not too many. I must make an early start in the morning."

Holmes' "early start", which I did not personally witness, was at six o'clock, by which time he had taken his usual light breakfast and left the house for the University.

I had hoped that his return that evening at eight boded well, especially as we still had no news at

Charlotte Square of Alexander's return. But it did not!

Having refused food, Holmes collapsed into a chair and began the silent contemplation of his fingertips, a preoccupation familiar enough to me, but one which I imagined was causing both Buchanan and McIntyre some discomfort. I suspect that they felt obliged to take their lead from me, to sit and wait until such time as it was Holmes' pleasure to break the silence! This, he did – after a full half hour.

"Filter off the dirt from the floor, and what is left is water, pure water – or as pure as any that's drunk in Edinburgh. There is no poison!"

"Holmes," I said, "I know that there's no-one more expert than yourself upon the subject of poisons. But you yourself said that this would be difficult. Forgive my suggesting it, but isn't it still possible that . . ."

"I've missed it! And there's nothing to forgive, Watson. Don't you think I haven't myself asked that same question? There are two men at the University not without some considerable skills in chemistry. I have had them check every one of my results. I've missed nothing. The liquid in those bottles is water – and nothing more!"

"But how is that possible?" McIntyre asked.

"There is an explanation – the same explanation why the boy, Alexander, has not returned."

Suddenly, I realised what that explanation was. Perhaps all of us in the room had seen it at that same moment, but it was Buchanan who spoke.

"Alexander has not returned because he has not failed. Holmes has found no poison because there is none. What happened at Amherst Street was carefully staged to deceive us. I had already been given the poison! And it is in me now!"

I looked at Holmes. His expression left me in no doubt that Buchanan had spoken the truth.

....

I have good reason vividly to remember the seven days which followed that evening. Buchanan, without the need for great persuasion, was induced to enter Edinburgh Infirmary, which offered, it seemed, not merely his best, but his only chance of survival. The very unusual, not to say bizarre circumstances of Buchanan's admission, coupled with the fact that both McIntyre's and my own examination of him showed him to be an apparently healthy man, could have led to difficulties. There were no difficulties. I must record here that whatever dislikes and clashes of personality there may have existed between Holmes and Dr Joseph Bell, at no time did either man allow those differences to interfere with his dedication to the welfare of Athol Buchanan. And I have no doubt that Joseph Bell, because of his position and the high regard in which he was held, used those advantages unsparingly, both to facilitate Holmes in his work and to provide Buchanan with the very best medical expertise that the Infirmary and the Medical School could provide.

Yet all of this seemed to be of no avail. Each night, I saw Holmes return to Charlotte Square, visibly more exhausted, visibly more despondent. Soon, I had stopped asking questions to which I already knew the answers. Holmes could still detect no poison in Buchanan's body. No medical examinations or tests had revealed anything in any way abnormal.

It was one week to the day since Holmes had sat in the same chair in which he now sat and made the dramatic announcement of what he clearly regarded as his failure. This evening, like those before it, had passed in relative silence. Holmes' sudden outburst was, therefore, at least unexpected.

"I cannot be so wrong! Whatever fiendish cunning it is that confounds us, it was conceived in the mind of man. What is conceived in the mind of one man can always be matched by the mind of another. This thing is not supernatural. Somewhere, somewhere along the line, my deduction has been faulty. Gentlemen. I crave your indulgence. Let us start again – from the beginning."

I had seen Holmes do this before. He would goad McIntyre and myself into fierce questioning of and argument about every small decision he had made or action he had taken. It was not done with the conviction that we would necessarily offer any new ideas, rather that it would force

Holmes himself into defending and, in so doing, re-examining his own thinking. Three hours of vigorous, sometimes heated, even ill-tempered, discussion, appeared to produce nothing new. It was now one in the morning. Holmes asked if he might be left alone with his pipe and his thoughts.

....

Something had happened during the night. Holmes was sitting at the breakfast table when I came downstairs. For the last week he had breakfasted and gone to the University two hours before I was even awake. He looked relaxed, almost cheerful.

Being Saturday, McIntyre had no surgery until that evening. Holmes had assumed that neither McIntyre nor I would therefore have any commitments, and that both of us would be available at ten o'clock. He was about to go out, but would return at a little before ten – with a carriage. Asked what were his intentions, he replied only that we were going to Queensferry.

The carriage duly arrived and I was slightly surprised to find in it, Mr McCrae, the man from the detective agency who I had met briefly at Amherst Street. Holmes introduced him to McIntyre.

"The reason for Mr McCrae's presence," he explained, "is a circumstance which has not, until now, appeared to be of any importance. You will remember, gentlemen, that Alexander was apparently fortunate in obtaining a ride for a part of his journey to Queensferry – on a coal cart. It was not 'fortune', but a situation which I had myself arranged. It was also not fortune that the cart, having reached its depot at Craiglieth, should meet up with another empty cart on its way to Queensferry. That second cart was driven by Mr McCrae."

"So!" McIntyre exclaimed, "you know where the boy, Alexander, went."

"Not quite," Holmes replied. "He asked to be set down at a spot which is very open, making it extremely difficult for Mr McCrae to carry out the task with which he had been assigned."

"I tried to follow him," McCrae said, "but I lost him."

"It is to that same spot that we are returning," Holmes continued. "I now believe that it could hold an answer for which I have not even been looking. Clearly, I cannot guarantee that we shall find it."

We stopped at a point on the road perhaps half a mile short of the still partly constructed Forth Railway Bridge, dismounted from the carriage and set off walking in the direction which Alexander had taken before McCrae had lost him. "Open" was an apt description of the area – some few trees and an almost total absence of buildings. Within two hundred yards, the land dipped and we could see the shoreline of the Forth. There were still no buildings, other than a derelict shed which might at one time have housed some kind of machinery. Some partly dismantled girderwork was still attached to one end of it.

"What's that?" Holmes asked.

"I'm told," McCrae answered, "that it originally housed pumping machinery. There was a lot of trouble with water when they started on the foundations for the approaches to the bridge. When its job was finished, they removed the machinery. The shed was used for a while to store drums of oil – but it's been empty for a couple of years, waiting to be demolished. If you're thinking that the boy might have gone there, I did look. You can walk into the place, but the floor's so dirty and greasy, you could hardly miss footprints – and I can assure you, Mr Holmes, there weren't any."

Holmes insisted on looking for himself. The floor was as McCrae had described it, but Holmes wasn't going to be content until we had entered the building and carried out a search, I couldn't think for what!

The place was larger than first impressions might have suggested, ill-lit, having no windows, but apparently empty except for some heaps of scrap metal and what I took to be empty oil drums. We had fanned out to make the search quicker. I had almost reached the end farthest from the doorway, and was stepping around some stacked drums, when Holmes' voice stopped me dead in my tracks – "Watson!" he shouted. "Don't move! Stand absolutely still where you are. And no-one else move any nearer!"

It was only seconds before Holmes had reached me and, for some reason, grabbed me firmly by the back of my coat. "Take one step backward, Watson. And now look down at where you were going."

Only then did I realise that what, in the half darkness, I had taken to be floor, was the edge of some kind of pit! Holmes had lit a lantern which he must have brought with him in the carriage. Its light showed a deep opening in the ground, perhaps twelve feet across and almost as wide.

"I assume," he said, "that it was needed to house some part of whatever machinery was here. You are very fortunate, my friend. But for that single shaft of light coming through the large gap in the woodwork of the back wall, even I might not have seen the edge of what you were about to walk into."

Holmes had directed the beam of his lantern downwards, but to little effect. "There's no immediate way of telling the depth," he said, "except that it's obviously a deal more than two or three feet. I see there's an iron ladder been fixed to the edge, though I wouldn't recommend using it. The fixing bolts look to be near rusted through."

McCrae and McIntyre had joined us. McCrae was also carrying a lantern, one which appeared to be a deal larger and more powerful than Holmes'. Both beams were now directed into the pit. For several seconds there was nothing but a stunned silence, perhaps because of a total disbelief in what we saw. It was McIntyre who first broke that silence.

"God! What is it? It looks like hair – long, white hair! The pit's full of it. And I'd swear it's moving – or there's something that's moving in it! In Heaven's name, Holmes, what is it?"

"Perhaps," Holmes answered, quietly, "you should rather ask, 'What was it?' What moves was once human. It *was* a gypsy boy named Alexander. I'd guess that one or both of his legs are broken. What is certain is that he is very near to death, almost unable to breathe and, if still conscious, suffering quite unimaginable agonies of fear and pain."

"We must get down to him!" I said.

"No, Watson!" Holmes had grasped my arm. "There's no help for the boy – other than death itself! I still know so very little about what is down there. But this, I do know. It could mean certain death to anyone who might enter that pit to try to save him. And it would be for nothing. You must believe me, Watson. You must all believe me. That boy cannot be saved!"

....

In reconstructing these cases, there have frequently been gaps in the original information. In order to preserve the continuity, it has sometimes been necessary to fill those gaps with what are, admittedly, nothing more than educated guesses.

There is good reason to believe that, unusually, one of Watson's notebooks did contain a very full and detailed

THE FORTH-BRIDGE.
LENGTH INCLUDING VIADUCT 8098 FT. = 616.
HEIGHT 369 FT SPANS 1710 FT. BEGUN (23RD JUNE 1883...

description of what happened at Queensferry on the morning of Saturday, October 27th 1888. What is certain, is that those pages have been carefully and deliberately torn out. What remains breaks off at the point in the text which has been reached, above.

Only one other clue exists to the events of that Saturday morning. In "The Scotsman" for Monday, October 29th, a brief reference is made to a fire which occurred at about noon on the previous Saturday, and "which gutted a disused wooden building just east of the southern approach to the Forth Bridge". The fire was thought to have been caused by spontaneous combustion, the building having last been used for storage of oil drums.

Accepting that the boy was dying, perhaps in agony, and beyond all help, and that what lay in the pit was potentially deadly, then three possible versions of what did occur, suggest themselves.

The first is so totally out of character with what we know of those present, that it can readily be dismissed. It is that the pit was deliberately set on fire with the boy still alive in it.

The second is that the boy was first killed as an act of mercy, before the fire was started. Watson habitually carried a revolver. It is possible that McCrae was also armed. Who might have actually fired the shot(s) is again a matter of pure speculation.

The third is that the fire was accidental. Holmes and McCrae both carried lanterns. Either could have dropped one of them.

In keeping with the practice of filling in gaps in information, with best guesses, the temptation would be to choose the third alternative as being the least controversial. But why did someone (Watson?) remove those pages from the notebook? That would suggest the second alternative but, without any actual evidence, it is an assumption which the author is not prepared to make.

Chapter Seven

The Deadly Dust

I have no doubt that all of us involved in this case could have wished that it might have ended in a manner less terrible than the awful thing we had witnessed at Queensferry. Sherlock Holmes had often shown himself to have stomach for many things which I had myself found sickening, but it was not until the evening of the Sunday which followed that dreadful Saturday, that he made any attempt to bring together the seemingly disconnected pieces which McIntyre and I now had in our minds.

I could well have understood that any satisfaction which Holmes might have felt in solving the mystery would be marred by the nature of the events which had brought it to an end. What I found surprising, was Holmes' certain annoyance at himself for failing to see what he described as "the obvious".

"It was all there," he said, "from the beginning. I should have seen it on that very first morning when you, Watson, told me the story of the Buchanan Curse. I should have known that whatever vengeance had been devised for the murder of the woman, Dya, it would be something peculiarly appropriate to the nature of the deed. Tradition demands that it should be so. And there lay the first clue – the woman strangled with her own white hair!

"But I missed it. More unforgivably, I missed it again when I came upon Hare's confession and the story of the Buchanan coffin, filled with white hair! I even saw what could have suggested the solution to me when you, Watson, mistook a piece of mouldy bread for a furry animal! 'Drab' isn't a poison. It's a rare mould. Its spores are like a fine dust. They can be given in food, suspended invisibly in a liquid – or even blown into the air which the victim will breathe. They grow in the lungs as hair-like threads which will quickly choke the victim to death – your 'phthisis' Watson. I found nothing in the water I took from the floor of the kitchen in Amherst Street because the spores were mixed with the dirt which I so carefully filtered off!

"Even when we went to Queensferry, I had still not realised that 'drab' was not a conventional poison, indeed was not a poison at all! The reason for our journey to Queensferry was a simple one. For days I had assumed that Alexander had not

returned to Amherst Street because he had succeeded. The night we talked and argued, going
over every detail of the case, I did, at last reach
one right conclusion – for the wrong reason! I supposed that I had found no poison because, unlikely
though it seemed, there was none. Alexander had,
in truth, failed. Therefore, the only reason that he
had not returned to Amherst Street must be that
he could not. I had remembered the injury to his
head and thought it might be more serious than I
had supposed. But it was not until we were *at*
Queensferry, when McCrae told us that the building had been used to store oil drums, that I first
connected it with the oily mud on the kitchen
floor. The rest came together only at the point
where we were stood looking at that scene of
horror in the pit."

Precisely how that horror had come about,
Holmes could only surmise. The evidence which
we had seen, and which I had recorded as it lay on
the kitchen floor, suggested that the boy might
have swallowed some of the water that must have
spilled over him from the jug. Holmes knew that
the boy might, therefore, have swallowed what
he then believed to be "poison" – but since it
would not kill immediately, that had not pre-
vented his return. It may have accounted for the
boy's leaving the house in some panic. It probably
accounted for what we had seen in the pit.

The disused building had provided the hiding-
place for the "drab". The boy had returned there,

entering through the hole broken in the back wall, and thus leaving no footprints. Somehow, he had fallen into the pit, breaking one or both legs. He had been unable to climb out. When he slipped and fell in the kitchen he had not only swallowed the spores, but his clothing became covered in them. Crawling about in the pit, perhaps rolling in agony in the oily dirt, he had spread the spores over a surface upon which they apparently thrive. They had grown everywhere, not only in the boy's lungs, but on his flesh and clothing, as well as the floor and walls of the pit wherever he had been in contact with them.

....

One thing remained to be done. We had to prove what *was* still theory even though it so clearly explained events. It was that which, one week later, brought Holmes, McIntyre, Buchanan, Dr Joseph Bell and myself to the chemical laboratories of the University Medical School. Holmes took us into a small room where five large, bell-shaped glass jars stood upon a work bench. Three of them were filled with what did have every appearance of white, human hair, some of it all of ten inches long.

"Fortunately," Holmes said, "by sheer chance, the 'dirt' which I had removed, had not been thrown away. What you see has been grown from the spores which were in it, in the space of just six days. You might prefer not to know, what on! Dr Williamson of Edinburgh's Botanic Gardens has finally succeeded in identifying it as the rare, exotic mould, *Mucor phycomyces*."

"The empty jars," I said, "have not grown?"

"They have," Holmes answered, "but last night were deprived of moisture."

"But the mould has completely vanished!"

"Not 'vanished', Watson. The hair-like structures – the hyphae – are gone, which is why no trace of anything unusual has been found in any victim after death. But they have left behind them millions of dust-like spores. It is only the spores which kill. So Burke and Hare suffered no harm from their discovery in the Calton Burial Ground, but the air in the pit at Queensferry might have been full of spores, and therefore deadly. I had no way of knowing."

"If this is 'drab'," McIntyre said, "how can so fine and deadly a dust be handled, and safely!"

"I can only guess," Holmes replied. "These spores can survive for many years. Perhaps they were mixed with some other harmless substance, like clay. When they were required to do their deadly work, it was necessary only to soak the mixture in water."

....

The next day, I returned to London. Holmes expressed a wish to stay on in Edinburgh with Buchanan, at least until the fateful day of November 9th, though I could see no real reason to think that Buchanan had anything further to fear. The last victim of the Buchanan Curse had been not Athol Buchanan, but rather his intended executioner! More than that, the true nature of the ancient "poison" was now known. The facts would be well recorded in every medical journal. "Drab" could, of course, be used again, but not without instant recognition of the quite unique symptoms – and therefore the probable apprehension of the murderer!

In the event, November 9th did prove itself to be a fateful day, though not for Athol Buchanan. In London, there was yet another "Ripper" murder. The victim, Mary Kelly, was killed in her own lodging. The mutilation of the whole of her body was sickeningly horrific.

Holmes did not return to London until the 20th of the month, offering no reason for his prolonged stay in Edinburgh. Time was to show that the killing of Mary Kelly was to be the last of the "Ripper" murders, though no-one was ever arrested for the crimes. Of Athol Buchanan, it remains only to say that in 1893, he married a wealthy widow and in 1895, they emigrated to the United States of America.